To Johnny Tundra —J.C.G.

To my brother, Kent —W.G.M.

Snow Bear
Jean Craighead George

PAINTINGS BY WENDELL MINOR

HYPERION BOOKS FOR CHILDREN

New York

One spring twilight, the frozen Arctic Ocean pushes up a huge block of ice near the shore. It looks like a ship.

Bessie Nivyek puts on her parka, her boots, and her mittens. She wants to climb aboard the ice ship and pretend she is sailing to beautiful places.

Vincent Nivyek, her brother, is hunting for food. He sees the bear tracks following his sister. Bessie is in danger. Mother polar bears kill people who threaten their cubs.

He follows the tracks.

Nanuq, the mother polar bear, smells Vincent and his gun. Snow Bear, her cub, is in danger. Humans kill bears.

Bessie goes one way around the ship.
Snow Bear goes the other way.
They meet on the far side.

Snow Bear licks Bessie's nose. Bessie hugs Snow Bear. He turns a somersault. Bessie turns a somersault. Snow Bear falls over backward. Bessie falls over backward. They sit up and look at each other.

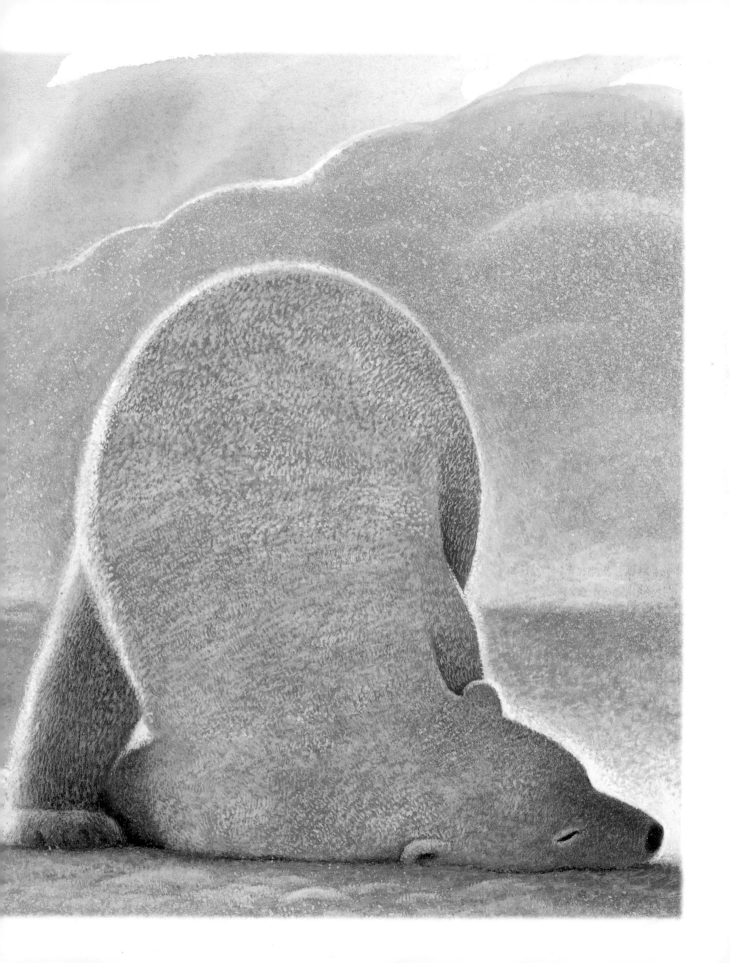

Up on the ice ship Vincent watches Bessie playing with Snow Bear. Little cubs are friendly. Up on the ice ship Nanuq watches Snow Bear playing with Bessie. Children are friendly.

Vincent looks for Nanuq.
Nanuq looks for Vincent.
Vincent remembers his father's words:
"The Arctic cannot be rushed. If we wait,
the answers will come."
Vincent waits.
Nanuq waits.

Snow Bear climbs up the ice ship. He flops on his belly and slides down to Bessie.

Bessie climbs. She slides down to Snow Bear.

Snow Bear runs in circles. His fur and his fat make him hot. He digs a snow cave and sits in it.

Bessie is cold. She sits beside Snow Bear.

Vincent waits.

Nanuq waits.

Bessie and Snow Bear wait.

The Arctic will not be rushed.

Inside the snow cave Bessie grows warmer.

Inside the snow cave Snow Bear grows cooler.

An enormous male polar bear rises up through a break in the ice. Nanuq sees him. He is more dangerous than Vincent. Male polar bears kill whatever moves—even polar bear cubs. She slides down to rescue Snow Bear.

Vincent sees the enormous bear.
He is more dangerous than a mother
bear with a cub.

Snow Bear sees the enormous bear.

Bessie sees the enormous bear.

The male bear smells Vincent's gun. He slides
back into the water.

Snow Bear and Bessie run back the way they came.

Nanuq and Snow Bear walk farther inland. They will eat sedges and lemmings until Snow Bear is so big no male bear will hurt him. Vincent and Bessie walk home to eat, go to school, and learn the wisdom of the Arctic like Eskimo children do.

The ice ship slides back into the water and sails away.

Wendell Minor wishes to thank Thomas D. Mangelsen for the use of his polar bear photographs as reference for the illustrations in this book.

Printed in Hong Kong by South China Printing Company Ltd.

First Edition

3 5 7 9 10 8 6 4 2

This book is set in Joanna 18-pt. type.

Library of Congress Cataloging-in-Publication Data:

George, Jean Craighead, 1919-

Snow Bear/Jean Craighead George; illustrated by Wendell Minor.—1st. ed.

p. cm.

Summary: Bessie and a polar bear cub named Snow Bear play on the ice, while her older brother and the mother bear watch to make sure that everyone is safe.

ISBN: 0-7868-0456-4 (trade)—ISBN: 0-7868-2398-4 (lib. bdg.)

[1. Polar bear—Fiction. 2. Bears—Fiction. 3. Play—Fiction. 4. Eskimos—Fiction. 5. Arctic regions—Fiction.] I. Minor, Wendell, ill. II. Title.

PZ7.G2933Sn 1999

[E]—dc21 98-46388